SKOKIE PUBLIC LIBRARY
Y0-DWO-644

# If I Were a TIGER

Tyger Tyger,
burning bright,
in the forests
of the night

written by
**Caroline Coleman**

**WATERBROOK**

illustrated by
**Nadya Bonten-Slenders**

**To my Luke, who loved his tiger costume in every season, and in memory of my beautiful daughter, Sheila**
—CAROLINE

**To my little Luky**
—NADYA

If I Were a Tiger

Text copyright © 2022 by Caroline Coleman
Cover art and interior illustrations copyright © 2022 by Nadya Bonten-Slenders

All rights reserved.

Published in the United States by WaterBrook, an imprint of Random House,
a division of Penguin Random House LLC.

WaterBrook® and its deer colophon are registered trademarks of
Penguin Random House LLC.

ISBN 978-0-593-23554-6
Ebook ISBN 978-0-593-23555-3

The Library of Congress catalog record is available at https://lccn.loc.gov/2021016912.

Printed in China

waterbrookmultnomah.com

10 9 8 7 6 5 4 3 2 1

First Edition

Book and cover design by Ashley Tucker

Special Sales Most WaterBrook books are available at special quantity discounts
when purchased in bulk by corporations, organizations, and special-interest groups.
Custom imprinting or excerpting can also be done to fit special needs. For information,
please email specialmarketscms@penguinrandomhouse.com.

Beyond the cave
of my cozy bed
there lies a world
that gives me dread.

Shadows slip beneath the door
and pad along my creaking floor.
In the dark, they take on shapes
of **tigers, bears,** and **hairy apes!**

Everything's dandy. I'm feeling carefree!
Nothing's the matter at all—not with me!

My name is **Tim Bone**, and I'm scared of the moon,

the yellow-winged owl,

and the wailing typhoon!

I can't wear my sneakers.
I'm afraid to go near them.
There are monsters inside.
I know 'cause I hear them.

I hide from the big kids.
I don't want to look dumb.
What if they say that
I once sucked my thumb?

When it's time for drama,
I pull out a book.
The curtains make
a cozy nook.

Recess is
a lot to swallow.
Under the slide
makes a secret hollow.

The swimming pool's crowded
with kids who could sink me.

Mom's golf ball could **bling-blang** a tree and unjoint me!

For dinner, Dad cooks a vegetable stew.
I dive for the floor. It's totally *ew*!

I have to do something to **conquer my fears**.
Otherwise I think I'll break out in tears.

I have a **big plan**, and I'm going to do it.
I'm becoming a tiger. That's all there is to it.

If I were a tiger,
I'd stalk through the night
and glare at the world
with my moon and star sight.

If I were a tiger,
I'd run toward lightning.
I'd **snarl** something awful
at anything frightening.

If I were a tiger,
I'd prowl through the trees
and whip my long tail
to make a big breeze.

in the **hot, steamy waters** of a pale blue lagoon.

If I were a tiger, I'd pick all the lilies
until I fell laughing, overcome by the sillies.

If I were a tiger,
I'd **never** wear shoes.
Orange and black
are the colors I'd choose.

If I were a tiger,
I'd eat **only** meats.
I'd turn up my whiskers
at carrots and beets.

If I were a tiger, I'd play with the cubs,

rolling and growling
and sneaking back rubs.

If I were a tiger,
I wouldn't be scared.

I'd **laugh** with the big cubs
with all my teeth bared.

If I were a tiger,
I'd live in a cave
and **no one** would think
that I wasn't brave!

If I were a tiger,
I'd sleep through the night,
even if vampires
sucked up the light.

I would be **fearsome** instead of all shivery.
I would be **carefree** instead of quite quivery.

BUT . . . if I were a tiger, I'd lose all my friends.
They'd run away shrieking to the earth's farthest ends.

My older brother
would not want to play.
Even my parents
would have nothing to say.

If I were a tiger,
I'd have to crawl.
And I couldn't take classes—
**not any at all!**

WILLIAM BLAKE
ELEMENTARY SCHOOL

Welcome
back

If I were a tiger, I couldn't slide to home base

or steer my sleek spaceship into deep outer space.

I couldn't tip on my toes or have jam with tea.
I couldn't sip honey made fresh by a bee.

I would be scary instead of all huggable.
I would be lonely instead of so lovable.

So instead of pretending
or hiding away,
I kneel, close my eyes,
and begin to pray.

I remember **God loves me**
and calms all my fears.
He holds my right hand
and **dries all my tears**.

God made the tigers, the moon, and the woods.
God formed the world and called it all good.

So if God made me special and chose every feature,
who am I to turn into a boy-eating creature?

Sometimes I still have a fear—or a **fright!**
But I know that it's going to come out all right.

God is my best friend
and helper, you see.
He gives me such peace,
and with Him, I'm **free**.

My name is Tim Bone, and you can join me
inside of my cave—or up in a tree.
Because if I were a tiger,
I'm starting to see . . .

the trouble is that I couldn't be ME!